For Aya, the best friend our family could imagine. —M.L.

To Max. I miss your face. —R.F.

THIS IS A BORZOI BOOK PUBLISHED BY ALFRED A. KNOPF

Text copyright © 2023 by Minh Lê
Illustrations copyright © 2023 by Raissa Figueroa

All rights reserved. Published in the United States by Alfred A. Knopf,
an imprint of Random House Children's Books, a division of
Penguin Random House LLC, New York.

Knopf, Borzoi Books, and the colophon are registered trademarks of
Penguin Random House LLC.

Visit us on the Web! rhcbooks.com

Educators and librarians, for a variety of teaching tools, visit us at
RHTeachersLibrarians.com

Library of Congress Cataloging-in-Publication Data is available upon request.
ISBN 978-0-593-37749-9 (trade) — ISBN 978-0-593-37750-5 (lib. bdg.) —
ISBN 978-0-593-37751-2 (ebook)

The text of this book is set in 16-point ITC Usherwood.
The illustrations were created digitally.
Book design by Nicole Gastonguay

MANUFACTURED IN CHINA
10 9 8 7 6 5 4 3 2 1
First Edition

Real to Me

Minh Lê • Raissa Figueroa

Alfred A. Knopf
New York

When you have a great friend,
the rest of the world can seem to disappear.

Others tried to tell me that she wasn't real,
that she was just imaginary.

But what did they know?

We laughed together,
were brave together,
got in trouble together,

and sometimes we were even quiet together.

My friend was always there for me,

and I can't imagine anything more real than that.

She was real to me.

Then one morning . . .

she was gone.

I thought maybe she got up early,
so I searched everywhere.

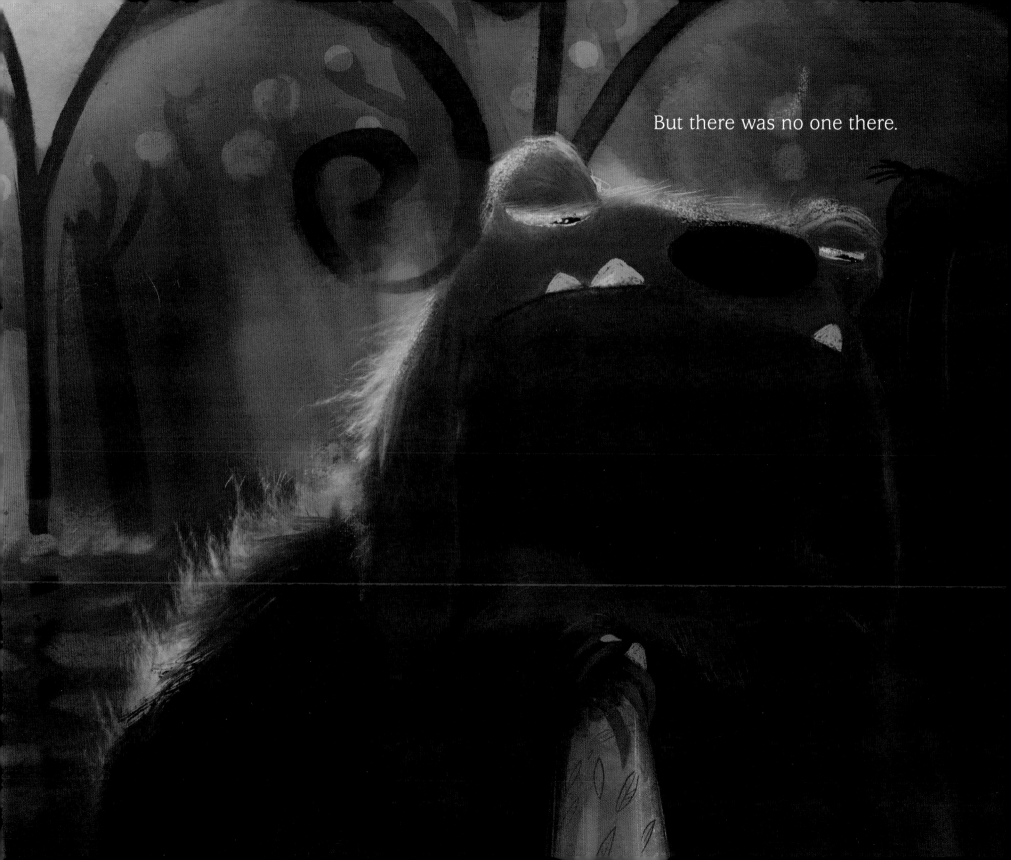

But there was no one there.

I couldn't imagine where she would have gone

without me.

Maybe the others were right all along.

Maybe I did just imagine her.

And yet . . .

I missed her laugh,
I missed her when I was scared,
I missed getting into trouble together,

and now that she was gone,
it was a little *too* quiet.

I missed my friend.
I can't imagine anything
more real than that.

She was real to *me*.

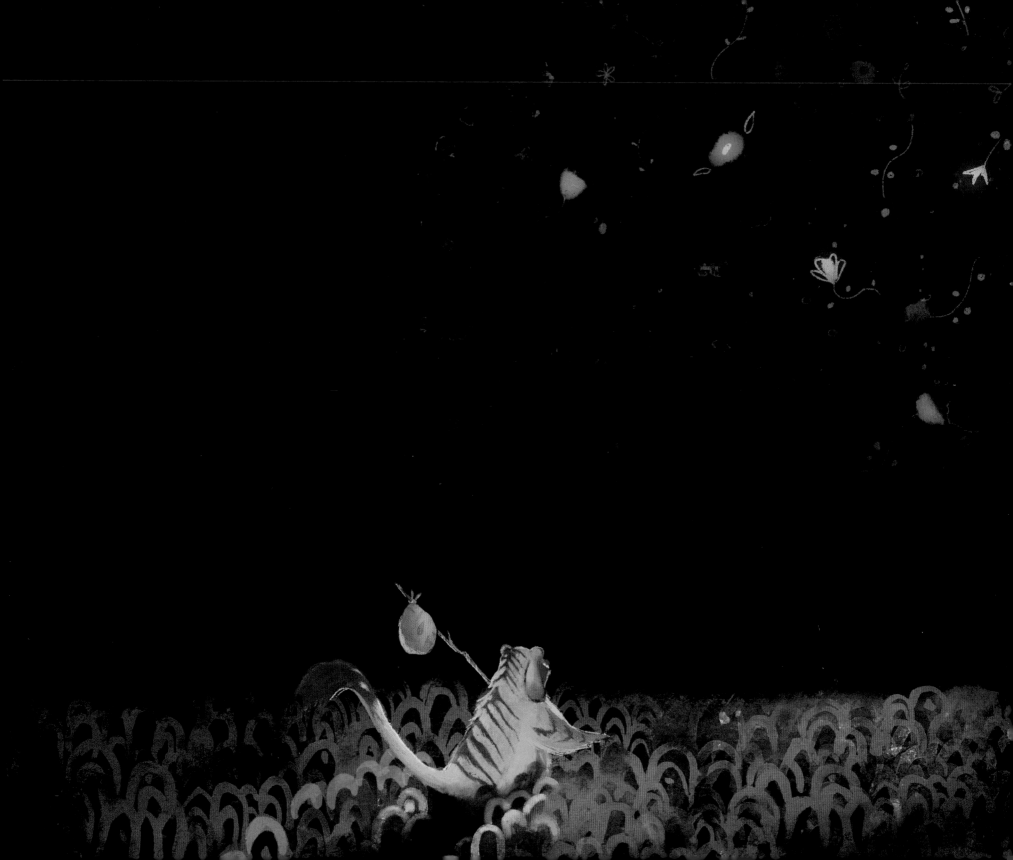

With time, I did make new friends,
and eventually . . .

we laughed together,
were brave together,
got into trouble together,

and sometimes
we were even quiet together.

When you have great friends,
the rest of the world can seem to disappear.

And while a lot of time has passed since I last saw her,
I still think about my first friend
and wonder what she's doing now.

I can only imagine.